VALLEY OF PROGRESS

THE
MURDE MOUNTAINS

ARCHIVE 1

Cory Sheldon

THE MURDE MOUNTAINS
VALLEY OF PROGRESS
ARCHIVE 1

Published by Ooi Iro

Illustrations by Cory Sheldon
Edited by Linda Cuckovich
Layout by Melissa Olson

Library of Congress Control Number: 2016911105

ISBN 978-0-9975692-1-6

www.valleyofprogress.com
twitter @valleyprogress
www.corysheldoncreative.com

FIRST EDITION

In Memory of Ross M.

Friend
Dreamer
Thinker
Believer

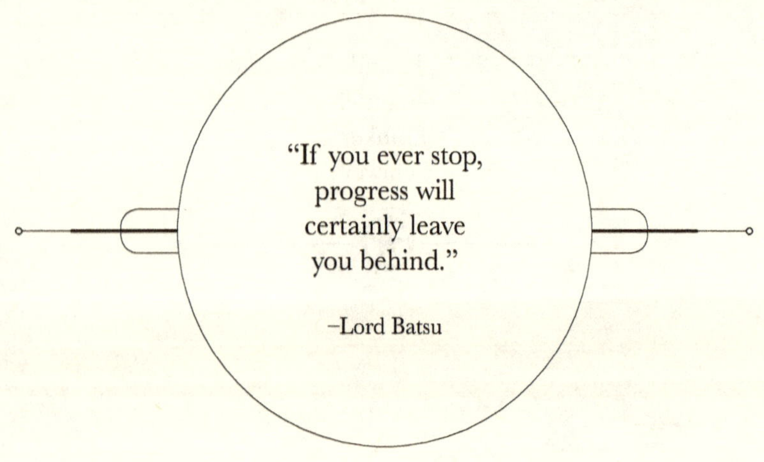

"If you ever stop,
progress will
certainly leave
you behind."

–Lord Batsu

PROLOGUE

The following are accounts collected, transcribed, and partially dramatized by Lord Rouk KaDela, G.A. in History from Meijune Academy. Individuals are accounted for and recalled based on all knowledge present to the author upon the time of the writing, and to the best of his ability.

In this recollection, you will witness the journey of Jean Batsu's pilgrimage west from Meijune into the Murde Mountains. The events and discussions are based on firsthand accounts, personal diaries, documents, and physical evidence. As with most of Lord KaDela's historical recollections, the information given is presented as a dramatic retelling in order to assist the reader in their empathy of the events, and create a more vibrant experience.

This recollection begins on the eastern base of the Murde Mountains, right at the location known as the Celestial Wall.

1
LIGHT

Every land possess a feature that stands out above all others, something that dictates development and births legends. An element of nature that has the ability to give life as well as take it away. Across the entire planet, nothing stood taller or stretched farther than the Murde mountain range. An impossibly massive wall of rock, it thrust out for over four-thousand miles as the two ends of the continent pushed into each other. At its narrowest points, its width could be crossed by a skilled team in a little over a week's time. For those unprepared, it would be common to not make it out at all.

Nearly every climate imaginable existed at some point along the entirety of the Murdes. At any moment the mountains could be yielding a massive snowfall in one area while breathing a scorching wind on another. Near the center of the range stood its tallest peaks, the tallest on the entire planet, an area known as the Celestial Wall. To most it stood as a majestic impasse that only the most audacious would ever dare attempt, a frozen ascent into the heavens.

People often described Jean Batsu as the most intrepid man in Meijune. An eccentric inventor who obsessed over the standards he set for himself. A rather lanky man, some described him as an insect, always scurrying around, doing some task or another, never resting. Most could recognize him easily from a custom vest containing a curious amount of pockets, filled with various gadgets of his own making. If ever asked about them, he would describe each in detail, one at a time.

Having spent most of his career in the city of Meijune, Batsu had gotten to a point where the familiarity of the coastal municipality began to feel stifling. The Great Western Expansion had already begun, leading many groups to pilgrimage away from the coast, and Batsu wanted to push farther than anyone. He longed to formulate a new society, one that would forever cultivate progress. Quickly, he assembled colonists to fill all of its needs. As rumors of his plans grew, so did neighboring urges to beat him to the prophesied, unknown promise land. A number of groups hastily ventured into the Murde Mountains, underestimating what it would require of them. It did not take long for the mountains to turn into a graveyard of ambitions.

As an individual, Jean Batsu received most of his attention from a rather staggering portfolio of inspiring inventions and the occasional outlandish remark. Industrialists often considered his creations as nothing more than fantastical fascinations to the public; however, there were enough commercial successes to let Batsu perpetuate his life of discovery. His first truly profitable invention was actually his most derivative, an improvement over someone else's visionary creation. Frustrated with its short shelf life, Batsu managed to vastly improve the time a photograph would last. Birthed not out of creative desires, the advancement served as a functional tool for documenting his ever-growing garden of industrial explorations.

While his technological prestige developed into nothing short of iconic, his social skills had a rather esoteric reputation. His persistent quirks led him to being viewed as a persona more than as a mere human being. It was that persona which convinced his group of artisans and idealists to follow him to a promised land, free from creative limitations. That same devotion also kept his followers from questioning the decision to cross over the Celestial Wall. Outside the group, most referred to the pilgrimage as an odyssey of madness.

Ninety-six crusaders declared their devotion to the vision. An intentionally comprehensive collection, it comprised skilled individuals who covered all of the aspects needed in developing a new city from scratch. Batsu described the opportunity as an honor, one that would grant those ambitious enough to become a part of recorded history. However, Batsu did not bother getting to know many of the members personally, and repeatedly emphasized that entry into the group was strictly voluntary.

Despite spending most of his time in a lab, or in his own head, Batsu still had the sense to bring a seasoned mountain guide into the wild. A matter-of-fact man, Toumou had iron fingers and a graying beard grown out of pragmatism. Upon first seeing the explorer, Batsu's eyes fixated on the adventurer's completely unique, sun-bleached hat. It looked as though the elements had gradually influenced its look more than the original craftsman. Batsu wondered how many expeditions it must have taken to transform it into such a thing.

Toumou joined Batsu's exodus on the notion that he would be recognized as the authority on all things travel and survival. Toumou had never much enjoyed the congestion of the city but liked the idea of having influence in a remotely established colony. He didn't bat his worn, deep-set eyes when Batsu suggested they travel directly through the Celestial Wall. Tomou possessed no doubt that he could successfully lead anyone robust enough to handle the journey. Whether the proposed group presented such conditioning was something the lifelong explorer had yet to determine.

While the group spent a day at the base of the Murdes preparing for their ascension into the unknown, Toumou decided to scout ahead by himself. The sheer scale of the mountain kept his endorphin levels high, and he found the terrain to be satisfyingly arduous. Toumou had only seen such towering majesty at a distance: rich grass turning into silver towers, topped with fog and ice. Traveling up the rocky inclines, navigating around large rocks, he saw the Murde Mountains as perfection, both in beauty and in feat.

When Toumou returned, Batsu approached him rather calmly, trying to hide his glow of anticipation. They both looked stoically towards the towering mountain, chins held high.

"The route looks good; we'll be clear on the first day," Toumou reported.

Batsu checked the time on his toki. "Are you ready to take that hat on its greatest odyssey yet?"

Toumou did not appear to be charmed by the question. "How well do you know these people?"

Batsu kept peering up at the mountain. "They all have abilities and experiences that will contribute rather well to the settlement."

Toumou then thought of narrow passes and individuals clinging to lifelines. "Do you know them by name?"

"Only the more critical members. Why do you ask?"

"This mountain might require more than what some of them have to give."

"Yes, well, I certainly hope for the best, but do not fear. I have redundancies in place; if we lose a few on the way there, I'll be fine with that."

Toumou leaned in. "But if people start dying, do you think everyone else will still be fine?"

Bringing his attention down from the towering horizon, Batsu finally looked Toumou in the eye. The unconventional inventor often found empathizing to be quite a chore, generally exiting any situation that demanded such a thing. However, wedged onto a treacherous path with nearly a hundred people, he knew that even one mental collapse could prove highly problematic.

"Have you explicitly assessed that some individuals in the convoy are not going to make it?" Batsu inquired. "There is one pair who brought a cart that I estimated may be to bulky for the climb."

Toumou joined him in gazing out over the crowd. "I believe I can get this group across, but that's what I say. Ultimately, it's the mountain that makes that decision."

Batsu nodded and went back to brief his convoy. While walking, he imagined them fulfilling the roles he had planned, components of a masterpiece on the verge of creation. Batsu then took high-ground immediately above the camp and gathered his flock. After reminding them of the expedition's logistics, he decided to apply the force that would push them through the challenging passage ahead.

"You have all decided to leave your home, a city of illumination that has now faded off the horizon. Tomorrow we begin our final leg on a journey towards a brighter light, a city that will be birthed out of innovation and progress. You have already shown your bravery by taking up the tools you have mastered and setting off to build in an unknown land. The city we create will define modernization and redefine what people think possible. The final ascent will be difficult, but the brilliance we will produce cannot have any other journey. We will make our mark in history, and you will be remembered for your part. Now rest, for the path ahead will require the best from all of us."

Batsu felt his talk had provided adequate motivation; he slept well that night.

° ° °

The first day up the mountain went by as Toumou expected. The group shared an energy springing out of their collective anticipation, lifted further by the incredible view few of them had ever seen before. Gaining altitude, they looked back towards where they had come from. It all appeared so still and distant, but their focus quickly got pulled away as they felt the Murdes begin to press down from above. The group continued their ascension, the ground shifted, and every step felt heavier than the one before.

While finding the narrowing path rather daunting, the pilgrims still followed Toumou with the dedication of links in a chain. A few of them had gathered an intellectual grasp of mountaineering, but all agreed that Toumou knew much more. He would constantly look back over the group as he led them forward. Some took it as a sign of encouragement while others thought he simply took inventory of who remained. As they rose, the view became even more breathtaking, as did the thinning atmosphere.

Despite a shared burden of fatigue, sleeping on the first night became surprisingly difficult for the group. The camp fell silent the minute everyone got settled in, but their restless minds continued to toil, ruminating about life decisions and the rocks stuck in their boots. In what seemed like minutes, the sun rose, and Toumou's deep voice tugged again at the human chain.

While everyone prepared their gear, Batsu briefed Toumou on an updated list he had created, prioritizing everyone and everything in the group. Batsu knew his unseasoned convoy of travelers had to pack as light as possible, but in establishing a new colony, certain needs required explicit consideration. The priority

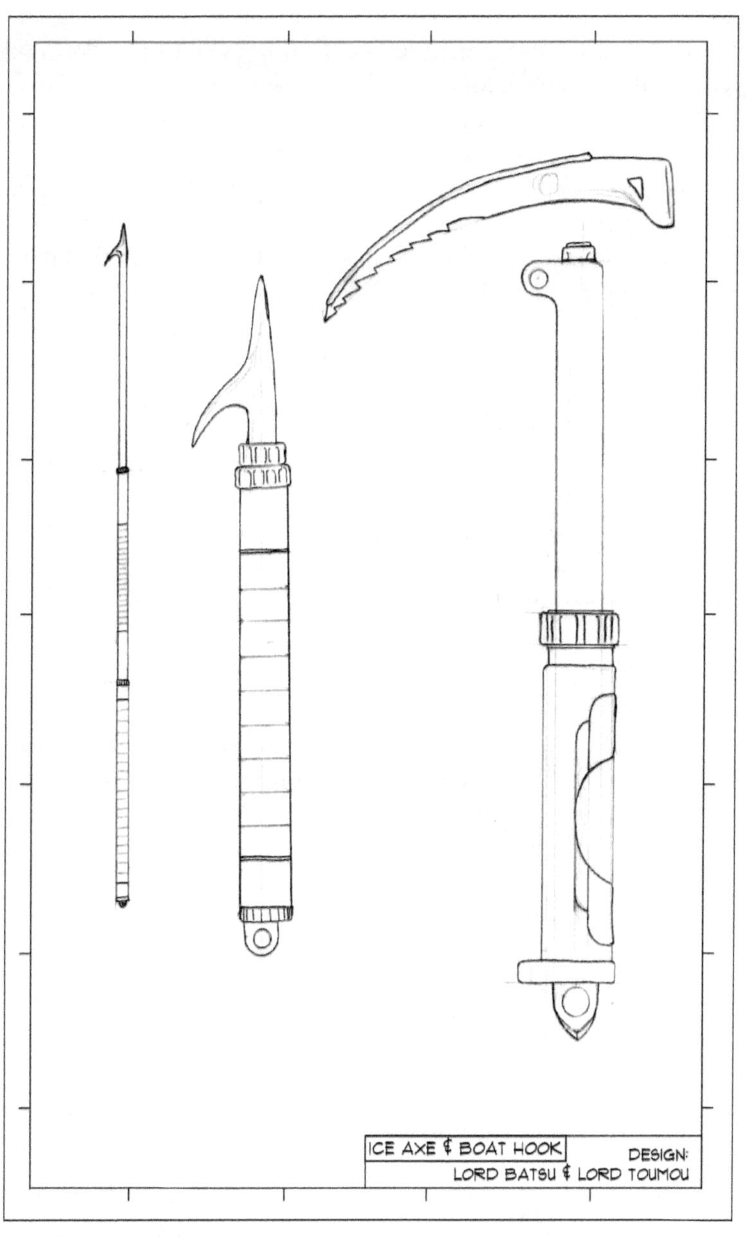

ICE AXE & BOAT HOOK
DESIGN:
LORD BATSU & LORD TOUMOU

lay not with carrying a surplus of rations but rather with tools that shaped natural resources into practical ones. Batsu understood that a box of nails had a finite life of usefulness, but metallurgy tools would produce as much as the artisan wished to create. Those responsible for surplus brought up the rear of the caravan.

The group finally reached their first critical obstacle, a narrow pass hugging the side of a curved rock wall. Despite being covered in snow, it had a magnificent view of a mountain spring, falling forty meters straight down. Up to that point, Toumou had held a constant pace, a challenging command providing a sense of security. So, when he fully stopped to evaluate the thin ledge, concern silently grew. Looking over the cliff, the group finally had a moment to appreciate that death now existed just a step away. The caravan that had been desperately gasping for air suddenly couldn't help but hold its breath.

Just where the narrow ledge began, Toumou anchored a braided rope by hammering a steel spike into the rock wall. A precious commodity at the time, Batsu had brought along both tools and minds necessary to create more steel; all positioned near the front of the line. Batsu got briefed by Toumou and then carefully headed down the convoy to prep everyone.

An intelligent metallurgist named Durbé arrived first to cross. Although a bit advanced in years, he proved more than capable of taking care of himself. Toumou wanted his heavy arms on the other side, stabilizing any uncertainty that arose. Durbé grabbed the anchored rope and tied a second around his waist, handing the opposite end off to Toumou, who braced himself. Durbé started to step around the bend, always keeping one foot in front of the other. His confidence maintained, but he kept in mind that any mistake could be fatal. He tried to ignore the trembling in his hand, hearing the water fall far below. When he reached the other side, he called out to Toumou with relief. Durbé then hammered in the other end of the rope, creating a sort of soft rail the others could brace on.

Durbé braced himself and tightly held the second line that Toumou, alternately, had tied around his own waist. In good time, he made it across and joined Durbé with an accomplished grin.

Toumou then transferred the second rope onto the main line, creating a larger loop just wide enough to fit around a pair of men.

"Lifeline," he said. He then tied on a smaller, third rope so the support loop could be pulled again to the front of the ledge.

Batsu returned to the front of the line, bringing along a willing woodworker named Martouk. The young man's soft face strained to remain confident while fighting a temptation to look down. Someone then handed Martouk a two meter boat hook, and on Toumou's command, he stretched it far over the edge of the cliff. Once he saw the hook appear around the curved rock wall, Toumou threw the pull line right towards it. Martouk saw the rope fly at him and instinctively lunged the pole out to grab it, his fore-foot sliding to the edge. The rope landed right on the hook, tipping the young man forward; gravity then started to take hold. Martouk's shifting weight wanted to take a small step forward, but the nearest ground sat forty meters below his foot. He felt himself start to fall.

Noticing Martouk's teetering, Batsu reached out and grabbed the end of the pole. In his rush, he had no time to get a good footing and got pulled forward. The two of them stood suspended like a high-wire act. Martouk looked straight down the cliff for what seemed like a lifetime. Batsu then managed to lean his weight back, pulling the two away from the drop. Martouk felt his center of gravity finally move back over his feet. He took a careful step away from the edge before turning towards Batsu, who saw eyes the size of fists.

"Watch your step, young man."

Air rushed into Martouk's lungs along with color back into his face. It felt like the closest he had ever been to death, even though the quiet affair had gone by unnoticed by the rest of the caravan.

"Back to work," Batsu said, with an unnervingly hard slap to the back.

The first pair in line tightened the straps on their gear. They put the secondary rope around their waists and grabbed the anchored main line. Hugging the wall, they started to move up the narrow pass as the rest of the caravan watched in complete silence. Every step executed with absolute focus; not even the ground they walked on was taken for granted, *especially* not the ground they walked on. Toumou and Durbé pulled in the secondary line as the pair made their way to the end, grabbing their hands as they finally met. Batsu counted, 4.2 percent down.

The system seemed to be working soundly, so Batsu decided to go across before some critical problem had time to arise. He called up another fit man to spot Martouk, a progressive-thinking farmer with a face full of sun-drawn freckles named Boro. Carrying very little weight, Batsu made it across the thin pass without complication. Toumou pulled him in and threw the rope back to Martouk. The rear of the line moved up.

As the rest of the caravan started to work its way across the intimidating ledge, Batsu took time to gaze up the mountain. The sounds of his flock began to fade away as he saw a curtain of clouds hiding the mountain's peak, a gateway to the future. Everything lay beyond that thick fog above him. Batsu felt progress pulling him onward. How appropriately challenging this journey was, Batsu thought, considering the prize that waited for him on the other side.

The fatigued travelers started to feel a buildup of confidence as the line reached its final pair. Hidden back behind the other end of the curved rock wall, however, such assured feelings did not exist. The final two pilgrims faced a fear that had been building since the group had encountered the narrowing ledge. A brother and sister team stood at the threshold, staring at a sickening irony. Just by looking at it, the O'wari siblings could see that their cart proved wider than the ledge. They had pushed their surplus of life support across countless miles, but now it looked like nothing more than an anchor that would pull them to their death.

Martouk hooked the rope that flew in from around the bend, making sure to keep his weight back. He and Boro began to strap the siblings into the loops on the secondary rope. A cool draft rose from the edge like a hand reaching for them from below. Looking around at the puzzle of space and gravity around her, the O'wari sister felt a thought shoveling into her mind; *this is not possible.* Her breathing became fast and heavy. She squirmed in her constricting space and began to panic. Her brother immediately picked up on her surfacing terror.

"Hey, it's okay, you'll be okay," he assured her.

"No, this is a bad idea."

Her brother reached out and gently put his hand on her shoulder. At first she failed to recognize it over the tension that crawled all over her skin. He gently grabbed her other shoulder.

"Everyone has already made it across. We'll make it, too. We will."

The brother immediately began to question the words he had just heard come out of his mouth, but it was of no consequence. They had made the decision weeks earlier; they were following Batsu all the way to the end.

"We'll give you all the support we can, but you can't let go of the line," Martouk added.

He stared at the siblings with absolute sincerity and gave the sister a firm pat on the back. He checked the rope's tension around the cart, hoping it would relieve the weight, knowing the outer wheels would inevitably go off the edge. Boro likewise tugged on the ropes as a final check and then nodded to Martouk.

"We're ready."

The O'wari brother gave his sister a nod; they started towards the cliff. Her first few steps felt solid as she slowly pulled the cart towards her. She rapidly shifted her eyes between the cliff's edge, the cart's wheel, and her brother's dead serious look of assurance. After two more small steps, the real test had begun: The outer wheel of the cart suddenly sat at the edge of the path that would only continue to taper in.

"Wait, wait!"

"What is it?"

"The wheel is going to go off the edge."

"We knew that was going to happen, Sis. It's okay. Just hold on to the rope and lean in."

The brother pulled the cart in towards the cliff so his sister could feel his support. She took a deep breath of cool air and started to pull the cart forward. As the wheel slipped off the edge, the sister could feel the cart begin to pull her away from the wall, away from what kept her alive. Her brother leaned in hard and tugged to counter gravity's grip pulling them towards the chasm below.

"I got it; keep going." His voice began to strain.

The siblings inched forward as blood flushed both of their faces. O'wari started to tense up his muscles as the rear wheel reached the edge of the cliff.

"Keep it tight," Martouk forcefully warned the other side.

As soon as the wheel went off the edge, the cart shifted away from the wall and all limbs tensed up. The combined effort of everyone on the line managed to stop gravity's heave, the siblings finding their bodies in the middle of a tug-of-war.

"Don't stop; just keep going!"

The sister nodded and continued to slide her feet around the wall. Toumou finally saw her appear around the bend.

"You're halfway there now."

It took everything the siblings had to keep the cart near the wall. It took the effort of every person on the line to keep the cart from going over the cliff, a reality they could all feel pulling without reprieve.

The sister could sense the fatigue start to build up in her hand as the cart seemed to get heavier. Through her sweat soaked glove she could feel the wood begin to slip. Willpower ceased to be the issue, knowing she had nearly reached her physical limit.

"It's starting to slip."

"Grab as tight as you can and keep going," her brother commanded.

"I can't hold it. We have to go back." Fire shot through her dying arm.

"We can't; we're almost there!"

O'wari looked up at his sister and saw the wood panel of the cart slipping through her waning grip. On her face he could see the fear of uncertainty being replaced with the terror of reality.

"Sis . . ." is all he managed to get out.

In an instant her hand flew up as the cart slipped from between her fingers. Everyone felt the shift, but their muscles had already hit the max. They had nothing left to give. The secondary rope popped up, the cart swiftly shifted down. The force of everyone on the rope caused it to catch a latch on the cart's side as Boro slipped onto the icy path. Toumou held his ground, aided by the steel anchor, but Martouk's strength couldn't manage. The sudden force of the cart caused the rope to burn through his hands like an arrow.

The secondary rope fixed the siblings to the cart while the O'wari brother, now alone in his efforts to hold the rear of the cart, got ripped from the wall. The cart flipped over and plummeted down, becoming gravity's prize. The sister could feel the secondary rope swing as her brother dropped off the edge. His weight hit her hard, and her grip with the main rope broke instantly.

Toumou braced for the siblings combined weight to challenge his position. Still falling below, O'wari saw his sister flip head first as the rope snapped tight, digging into his underarms. Coming out of the fog below, sounds of the cart smashing against jagged rock echoed back up. The big men on the line jerked forward but fought to keep their feet on the ground; the steel anchor pin bent forward. The sister screamed as the rope snapped tight. The line then cut into her waist before bouncing her body back up. On the rebound she spun and suddenly felt the rope slip down her legs. In a single gasp, she was free-falling.

The brother looked up to see his sister plummeting down with her arms stretched out. Time froze for a moment; nothing existed but the rope and his sister, who descended right past him. Although merely an instant, he saw straight into her eyes, so clearly as if they stood still. Neurons then exploded and his arm reached out. Her wrist crashed into his hand. He squeezed hard, the force of her weight swinging his arm down violently. Their limbs stretched out and a snap echoed up the mountain. O'wari's sister dangled below him screaming, her arm well out of its socket.

There should have been nothing left in him, nothing after losing the struggle with the cart. With his sister crying in pain, the brother somehow managed to pull her up to his level as if she were a small child. Some would declare it a miracle. Batsu would insist on an immense rush of endorphins and adrenaline.

"Put your arm around me." His voice demanded obedience. She did not argue and put her good arm around his neck.

"Get us out of here," he said, looking up.

The group above that had stood in shock watching the brother's miraculous display, suddenly snapped to.

"Pull 'em up!"

Toumou and Durbé impressively pulled in perfect sync as another jumped on the line to assist. The siblings floated up to the edge. The sister's face was filled with pain, her eyes shut like those of a frightened child. The brother held her tight.

"Pull 'em over. Watch her arm."

Another two men stepped up and rolled the siblings up over the edge, the sister crying and exhausted. The renowned physician Poel Jastoú, with a calm face and perfectly combed hair, followed Batsu down towards the O'wari pair. The brother sat up and looked over the edge. It looked peaceful. Batsu stood next to them as Jastoú bent down to the sister.

"It's her right arm," O'wari said as Batsu offered him his hand.

"Jastoú is a great physician. Your sister will heal."

The brother took Batsu's hand and stood up, giving no other gesture of gratitude. A mix of emotions swirled about his mind, but more than anything, he felt peace knowing his sister was safe.

"The mountain challenged you today and you won," Batsu said, patting O'wari's shoulder.

The brother thought of a few sharp comebacks but kept them to himself. He watched as Batsu made his way up the path to the front of the line, checking the status of the caravan along the way. O'wari gave Batsu a wary glance, wondering if they were chasing a promised dream (if such a thing could be promised) or just some psychotic ambition.

From a distance, Batsu had many attractive qualities; the size of the caravan presented proof enough of that. For many, including O'wari, his vision became a carrot too tempting to resist. Up in the mountains, however, the brother felt such ideologies and concepts starting to strip away. O'wari once thought Batsu could give him more than he could possibly imagine. Looking down, he wondered if it might cost him that which he considered most precious.

Kneeling back down to her, O'wari gently put his hand on his sister's cheek. She managed the faintest of smiles and closed her eyes. Around the corner, Martouk's voice shot out.

"Is someone going to throw the rope back?"

o o o

Camp set up quickly that night, and for those who kept the O'wari siblings away from a chilly grave, falling asleep became effortless. But for those who stood and watched out of arm's reach, their weariness could not overcome what the day's nightmare had left in their minds. Most of them lay awake replaying the events, picturing themselves going across that ledge that nearly claimed two of their fellow travelers. Death already breathed down their necks, and only two days into the climb, they knew it could last at least another week, maybe two.

o o o

Toumou got up with the sun and scouted ahead. The day before had only reinforced the importance of anticipating a mountain that offered very little grace. Getting stuck in the middle of a bad plan could prove devastating, but he also knew they didn't have a surplus of time to be cautious; every day on the mountain cost them. With the most cumbersome cargo already splattered at the bottom of a cliff, he decided to pick up the pace.

On Toumou's command, the group fastened up their gear, fought off the aches, and continued their journey upwards. The third day grew long. Only the position of the sun and the slope of the ground appeared to change. Sound seemed to disappear along with the flat ground far below. No one had the energy or motivation to speak, aside from the occasional murmur of ailments. Energy quickly became a precious commodity.

o o o

Day number four felt arduously similar to the one before, only inch by inch, everything became more difficult. No reprieve came from the biting air that seemed to somehow cool twice as fast as they ascended. Stiff muscles strained. Sensation began to leave their hands. The body felt like an old machine not allowed to turn off. Toumou continued on, pulling the exhausted line of people with the consistency of the passing sun.

Batsu tried to preach diligence, quietly enduring the effects of the mountain himself. The long days allowed for thoughts to wander. Even his own focused mind managed to slip off track under the wearying conditions. Batsu, along with everyone else, desperately longed to reach the summit of that frozen tower. The thought of simply going down became exhaustingly seductive. That intermittent goal, however, offered only a flirtation with success as the entire trek would likely last four times as long. Batsu started to question if his ambition had perhaps gotten the best of his planning. The assured man wanted verification.

"How long before we crest over to the other side?"

Toumou turned to Batsu, who stood rather close. He then sized up the path disappearing into the frozen fog. "Day after tomorrow."

Batsu heard no tone of concern in Toumou's voice. Verification enough.

∘ ∘ ∘

When Poel Jastoú ended his notable career, most considered him the most pioneering physician of the time. His discoveries allowed for a number of advancements that not only saved lives, but also accelerated the rate at which society advanced around him. One of his most notable areas of study was how the human body reacted to working in high altitudes. Thinning air, snow blindness, altitude acclimation; Jastoú would dissect and address all of those problems. Promptly on the fifth day of the climb, his desire to study all of them birthed.

The caravan had made its way up into a thick level of fog, a misleading sight considering the thin amount of oxygen present. Batsu began to feel desperation creeping up from his feet, crawling through his entire body. He conferred with both Toumou and Jastoú to evaluate the condition of the group, continuing to get slower the higher they reached. Toumou had never journeyed to that altitude before, and Jastoú's evaluations were nothing more than educated guesses at that point. They all agreed, however, that the Murdes slowly sucked the life out of them all.

Jastoú dropped back to the middle of the group, making sure no one wavered on the verge of collapse and threatened to compromise the line. The first potential candidate became an urban designer by the name of Pano. A neighboring man said he had been going on for thirty minutes, rambling about some cat he saw following them from up above. Pano said he fet nauseated and his face looked pale, but considering how anemic everyone looked, ghostly skin seemed less concerning.

"I think you may be hallucinating, Pano."

"Did you not see the cat?"

Jastoú got out a water canteen, opened it, and handed it to Pano. "Drink a third of that."

He didn't argue. Any form of rest by that point felt like a holiday. Pano took a few big gulps, wiped his mouth, and then shot a serious look.

"You should be careful with this, and especially our food. I think that's what the cat is after. I'm really hungry."

Jastoú paused for a moment, then reached into his medicinal alternatives bag and handed Pano two Oki leaves. A plant that Jastoú had recently discovered, it stimulated one's awareness.

"Chew on these for a while. I'll come back to see how you are doing."

Pano tossed them in his mouth and his face immediately turned sour, fighting an impulse to spit them back out. "Haven't you got any therapeutic smoked meats?"

"Don't eat it."

"Don't worry."

Feeling that there might be others on the verge of crossing the river of sanity, Jastoú continued down his line of traveling patients. Having seen Pano's quick-mountain-exam, Toumou suspected there had to be some other weak links on the line. It couldn't be long before their identities became obvious.

The fog continued to be an eerie sight, but it managed to foster an unexpected feeling of comfort. Limited visibility kept the group from seeing the daunting mountain bearing down on them, or the deadly drop always waiting patiently just a step away. Nearly all of them would claim to be enemies of ignorance, but with their bodies breaking down, most gladly allowed Toumou to carry the worries of their surroundings.

Looking ahead, Toumou grunted quietly as he saw the path begin to narrow. Despite no longer having the burden of the oversized cart, he wanted to avoid any narrow ledges if possible. He then saw a small rock wall ahead that slanted up to what looked like a possible alternate path. The sloped surface seemed a risky proposition for the caravan, but he figured that scouting it out would provide a better vantage point for either route. Toumou halted the line and signaled for Batsu.

"I'm going to take a quick look up there. We have path options, but neither is going to be easy."

Batsu nodded as Toumou handed Durbé a line with an anchor spike. No stranger to handling metal, Durbé quickly hammered the steel into the rock as Toumou tied a small harness around himself. Everyone in the group gladly rested as they watched him begin his steep ascent. The slight slant of the climb helped Toumou's tiring arms manage the ascension smoothly.

An aficionado of climbing, the explorer took up Batsu's offer to help build a light-weight, collapsible ice axe before they left. It seemed rather unnecessary at first, but at that altitude, Toumou started to feel grateful for any advantage. Finally gripping the top ledge with the new tool, he pulled himself up and caught a glimpse of something that made him stop dead still.

In a tight bundle only two meters ahead lay two white Ice Cat cubs. Toumou stood there, motionless, watching their small lungs rise and fall in a nest of brush. Unsure of why their guide had stopped, the group watched from below, none more concerned than Batsu.

The thin air had slowed Toumou's mind. He took a deep breath, finally gaining his sense to look down the path past the cubs. He noticed the passage looked sufficiently wide, lacking the narrow cliff of the alternate route; he just had to get everyone up there. While weighing the options presented to him, an uneasy feeling pulsed within. His determination to quickly evaluate the best path led him to dismiss the cubs as mere distractions; a grave mistake.

Before his next heartbeat, an adult Ice Cat leapt from the fog above and slashed its claws across his face. Toumou fell back from the wall towards the anxious group below. His wide back smashed into Durbé, the force bouncing him right off the cliff. Durbé yelled out as he clawed through the fog, then disappeared. Toumou bounced hard and then rolled off the cliff as Batsu reached for him in vain. Toumou fell before the lifeline snapped tight, jerking both the anchor and his bleeding head.

The group stood in shock as Toumou's groaning body dangled seven meters below. Batsu and a few others jumped on the line and immediately started to pull up their disabled guide. Everything had happened so fast, the entire group managed to miss what had caused Toumou to inadvertently kill his comrade. Batsu quickly dug into his pack and pulled out a compact steel winch of his own design.

"Give me some slack!"

The men on the line pulled up on sizable Toumou, who, along with his pack, pushed 350 pounds.

"More," Batsu commanded, his panicked fingers fighting the intricate device.

The men strained to give a few more inches, just enough. Batsu finally threaded the rope through the winch's lower guide and locked it down. He immediately began to crank the handle. Toumou smoothly started to ascend as the men pulling noticed their efforts becoming unnecessary. One of them noticed the rope grinding against the rock's edge. Quickly, he scrambled for a rounded shovel and slipped it in between them.

Away from the panic up at the front, a sound started to cut through the fog near the middle of the caravan. Tamak, who lugged a store of preserved meat, heard the low frequency resonance of what sounded like a motor. He looked up into the fog. The sound got louder, but nothing appeared. He looked over to his apprentice butcher, RóMean, whose head slowly turned up towards the sound. RóMean looked back towards Tamak to confirm that the sound really existed. A second later, the powerful white form of a Shiroku leapt down and vaulted Tamak off the ledge. His screams quickly vanished, along with his body.

Turning towards RóMean, the Ice Cat bared its teeth and let out a roar that stole the breath of everyone in the line. It lunged towards RóMean, who rolled up against the corner of the wall, desperately fearing for his life. The lion bit hard into the backpack containing more preserved meat. It flung RóMean out over the ledge, his body hovering over the deadly descent, and then back into the wall. He slipped out of the backpack as his face smacked against the rock. With the food for its cubs well in its jaws, the Shiroku shot forward towards the front of the line. Everyone dropped to the ground, covering their faces, and praying the fierce predator would pass them by.

Near the front of the line a confused textile artist named Tiké screamed in fear as the beast shot out of the fog. Before she could manage a place on the wall, the Ice Cat knocked her to the edge as it ran past. Gravity pulled on Tiké's heavy pack as her husband saw them disappear over the cliff. He lunged forward and reached blindly. Looking down, he saw his wife swaying below him, her sleeve slipping in his thick glove. Another pilgrim jumped towards them to help pull her up.

The Shiroku swiftly ran towards the front of the group, making off with its meal. Batsu, who was still pulling Toumou up from below the cliff, turned to see the Ice Cat rushing right towards him. He let go of the rope and reached for his revolver. Toumou dropped a meter as the other man braced him. Trying to track the cat's fast movement, Batsu raised the barrel of his gun and fired. The round grazed the beast, whose stride did not break for even a step. Batsu pulled back the hammer on the gun as the cat leapt towards him; he was too slow. The cat launched off of his shoulder, its claws pushing Batsu's arm down as a second shot was heard. In an instant, the Shiroku ascended the wall, hidden within the veil of fog.

Batsu looked down and saw blood on the ground; the second shot had gone right through his left thigh. It looked surreal, his shock fading out the sounds around him. Looking past his leg, he saw the other men finally pull the motionless Toumou up over the ledge, his face coated with blood. Jastoú, who luckily for the group had been at the back of the caravan during the attack, ran up to the two injured men. Batsu finally looked up from his bleeding leg to see the broken caravan trying to collect itself. Muffled sounds of moans and crying seeped through the fog. Days before, Batsu felt nothing but confidence as his group took its first steps up the Murde's east face. That night, he lay awake contemplating the dead, wondering if his only guide through the mountains would be among them by morning.

They took cover as best they could, knowing they slept at the mercy of the mountain and its guardian.

o o o

Diffusing through the fog, the morning sun gently woke the weary caravan. Half had succumbed to exhaustion and slept fairly, while others failed to overcome a night of anxious listening, waiting for the Shiroku to reappear. Jastoú spent most of the night tending to the wounds of the flock. Toumou's face, along with Batsu's leg, managed to occupy most of his time, but both seemed stable by sunlight. Jastoú felt exhausted to the point of nausea but fought through the pain, knowing that the group could not afford to lose either of its leaders.

Waiting for the rest of his group to rise, Batsu finally managed to get on his feet. Internally, he willingly took the injury as an excuse to catch some extra rest. His leg felt sore, but Jastoú concluded he lucked out with mostly tissue damage; he could walk on it, or at least limp. Batsu slowly made his way over to Toumou, finally seeing the guide's injuries fully illuminated. The image of what he saw changed Batsu's mood for the rest of their journey up the mountain.

Toumou looked at least as weak as anyone else in the group. One of his eyes hid behind bandages, which Jastoú said was too swollen to know if Toumou would ever see out of it again. A sling cradled his arm like a mother would hold an infant, a sign of fragility that looked rather grotesque on such a man. The overseeing father of the group had fallen and Batsu felt like an orphan.

"How is the arm?"

Toumou opened his free eye while rolling his head towards Batsu. "Doc said it's just sprained."

Batsu knelt down and gestured to Jastoú's assistant, who was cleaning up a few remaining cuts on Toumou's face. Understanding the hint, she handed Batsu the cloth and walked off.

"Are you going to be able to walk?" Batsu asked quietly.

"I landed upside down, so my legs are fine."

Batsu took a long breath. "Durbé is gone."

Toumou looked off the side of the cliff. "He was a good man. We owe him."

Batsu nodded in agreement. "So, we're not looking our prettiest at the moment."

"Speak for yourself," Toumou said through blood-crusted lips as he looked over Batsu's beaten body.

"So getting mauled by an Ice Cat is all it takes to bring out your sense of humor?"

"It'll go away."

Batsu got up and reached out his hand to the injured guide. As Toumou slowly stood, he gritted his teeth and let out a groan. Perpetually determined, he eventually stood tall. Batsu leaned towards him while looking down the line.

"Do you think this group can do this three times over?"

Toumou joined the evaluation before looking straight into Batsu's eyes. "Probably not all, but I can still get most of us out of here."

"I'll get someone else to spot you. Who do you want?"

"Someone smart enough to take care of himself, but not so smart he'll question what I tell him to do."

"I'll go get Martouk," Batsu said, then went down to find him.

The caravan gathered its gear and got back in line. With Martouk at his side, Toumou charged forward through the narrow passage below the Shiroku's den. Every set of eyes nervously looked up into the fog as they passed the home of the killer cat. Batsu stayed close to Toumou, whose pace was noticeably slower. The tempered speed felt easier on their bodies, but silently, many worried it would keep them from ever leaving the mountains.

Eventually the group did gain a bit of momentum, encountering heavier fog the higher up they went. It became so thick that all anyone could see was the bobbing backpack directly in front of them. Losing focus on their greater cause, many became entranced with the portable packs, memorizing every detail down to the fine stitching. The ground passing below their feet became hypnotic. Minutes felt like hours. As oxygen continued to thin out, it became hard to focus. Some minds would fade out, only to resurface with disappointment that they hadn't woken up in their bed back east. Up ahead, Batsu kept a close eye on Toumou; he could not afford to lose their best chance of getting out of the mountains.

"Do you think we're good on this route?"

Toumou continued onward, looking down what little path he could see with his one good eye. Batsu waited a moment. No response.

"Toumou," Batsu said discreetly.

"This is a good route," Toumou placidly responded.

Batsu stayed fixed on Toumou, who continued to look into the gray void. "How are you holding up?"

Again, no reply. Although generally not a man of many words, Toumou rarely seemed explicitly withholding. Batsu found no contentment with the silence. "Toumou, if you're not doing well I need to know."

"You'll follow anything I say as long as I have the breath to say it. What does it matter how well I am doing?"

Batsu did not know whether to take the words as an insult or an observation. Either way, it became clear that wishful thinking had vanished back down the mountain. Batsu slowed his pace and watched Toumou go off into the fog, into uncertainty. Quietly the caravan followed Toumou like an army of ghosts marching in limbo. The road ahead looked indistinguishable from the path behind, and the fog made it impossible to know the location of the sun. Even if Batsu knew his destination, he had no idea when he and his dedicated clan would arrive, if they would arrive at all.

Batsu watched the procession pass by until Jastoú appeared through the gray, asking a young man some questions. Jastoú saw the concern on Batsu's face and sent the young man onward. Batsu and the doctor followed right behind.

"How is the leg?"

"Under normal conditions I'd be complaining about it all day. As it were . . ." Batsu shrugged.

"How is Toumou holding up?" Jastoú asked with his thinning voice.

"I think a second opinion is needed."

The pair headed back up the path, passing the drained travelers one by one, embraced with equable cold. Ice existed everywhere now, a practical motivator to keep one moving to feel warm. Before reaching Toumou, Jastoú and Batsu noticed a man bent over on the ground, holding up the group.

The physician hurried to him. "What's wrong?"

"He was saying his head hurt, and he felt sick," the woman standing over them answered.

The man's ghostly face looked dreadful. Jastoú tilted his patient's head to look into his eyes. Suddenly the man convulsed and spun his face towards the ground. He started to vomit but hardly anything came out.

"Get me some water," Jastoú commanded.

The woman reached for the fallen man's canteen. Jastoú knew dehydration could be an issue on any long trip, and vomiting would only accelerate the problem. Batsu turned to an onlooker. "Go get the pop-stretcher."

The man started to run but quickly stopped and turned back around. "Wait, who has it?"

Remembering the face but never having bothered to learn the name, Batsu deferred to Jastoú, who said, "It's Jade. She's behind us."

As the man ran off, the new patient stopped heaving, and Jastoú reexamined his eyes. Having seen similar symptoms develop recently with others, he began to suspect that the high altitude directly contributed to the deteriorating health of the group. Jastoú noticed that it became incredibly difficult to catch one's breath, even after resting. He thought of ways to neutralize the rapidly spreading symptoms, but if a lack of breathable air was truly the culprit, he knew exiting the mountain presented their only hope.

Holding a bundle of metal and fabric, Jade ran up to Batsu, who signaled the young apprentice to hand him one of the two exposed handles on the pop-stretcher. As they pulled in opposite directions, the bundle unfolded in a dance of gears and clicks. The stretcher brilliantly locked into its final form: a rigid frame with a fabric bed and single wheel that lowered to the ground.

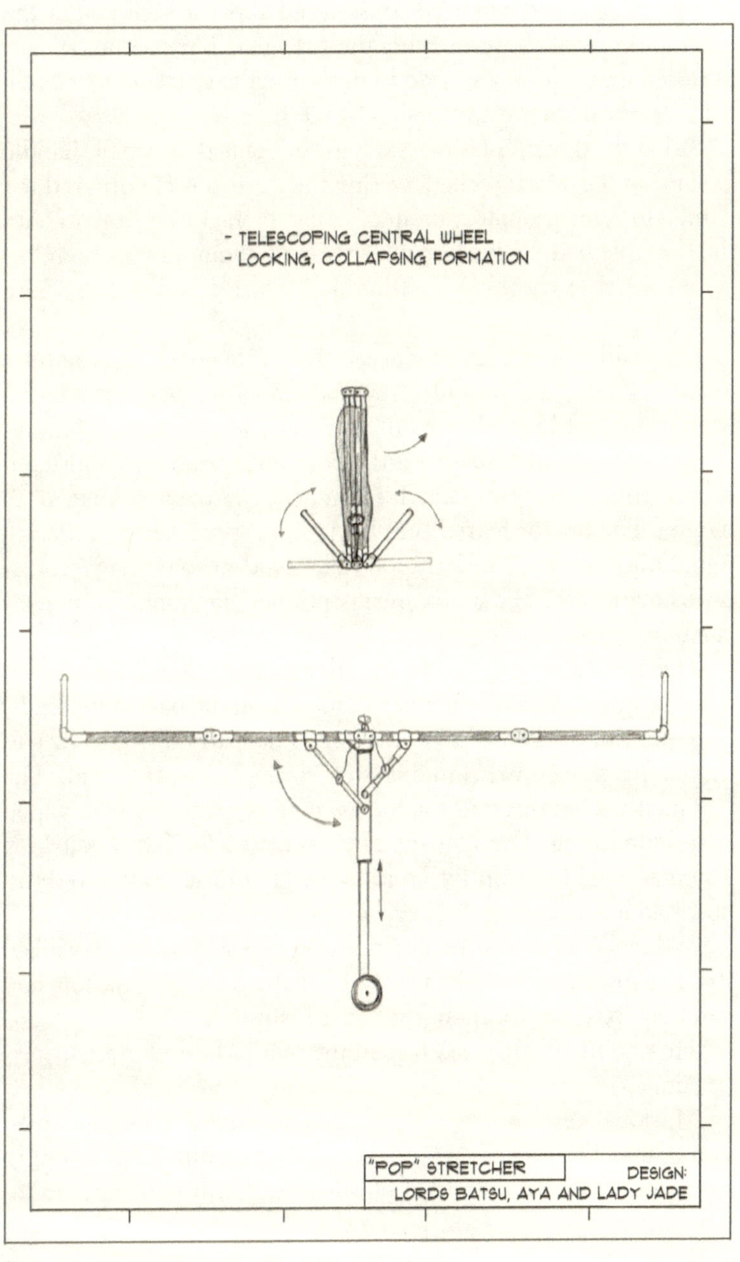

- TELESCOPING CENTRAL WHEEL
- LOCKING, COLLAPSING FORMATION
"POP" STRETCHER
DESIGN:
LORDS BATSU, AYA AND LADY JADE

Its light weight and balanced stress points kept the strain off of the patient as well as those carrying the stretcher. The technologically obsessed group took a second to marvel at the stretcher's first real field test—a collaborative design by all three.

"Bring it down," Jastoú said as he pulled a small handle, collapsing the wheel while lowering the stretcher. He ordered the ill man to drink a small amount of water, then guided him up onto the portable bed. "Give him a bit more in about half an hour."

"We need to catch up to Toumou," Batsu reminded the both of them.

Even with his leg injured, Batsu did about as good as anyone else. As they walked, Jastoú again reminded him of his luck, considering what didn't get hit with the bullet. Feeling less fortunate, Jastoú's body continued to wane from the constant care he administered to everyone else, although his panache partially managed to hide it. The doctor feared that his fatigue, especially considering the altitude they seemed trapped in, could become dangerously problematic. Still, the weary men continued on, hoping to quickly catch up.

The gap caused by the ill man proved larger than they realized. They saw no one. Both men began to pick up the pace until finally something appeared out of the fog. The pair slowed down as they noticed a crowd standing still, staring straight ahead. The two men waded through the lifeless pool of pilgrims, who gaped into the nothing. The halt signaled an alarm for Batsu, knowing Toumou wouldn't stop for good news. He quickly wondered just how bad it was.

Suddenly Martouk emerged through the mist and walked straight towards him. He limply held the arm sling Jastoú had carefully fixed on Toumou just hours before.

"He said he had to work something out," Martouk stated.

"Alone?"

Martouk gestured down the path to where Batsu assumed Toumou still remained. The dependable, veteran scout began to bring an uncomfortable level of surprise. Batsu tried to hide his growing fear.

"Give me a minute. I'll call for you."

As Batsu walked into the ocean of fog, a hammering sound started to emerge. His mind raced with images of Toumou starting to lose grip on reality until the lost man physically appeared. The first level ground Batsu had felt since on the mountain trailed off to the left, into an unknown path. The right edge dropped off below, creating a one-meter gap between the trail and a towering ice-wall that shot straight up. Toumou had just finished hammering an anchor into the ice, then preparing a harness.

Batsu cautiously took a few steps closer and pointed to the left. "Does that path dead end?"

"Doesn't matter. It doesn't go up," Toumou replied, his eyes examining the ice. He spoke with such composure that Batsu nearly missed the rather obvious question.

"We do eventually want to start heading back down, though. How do we know we're not peaking over?" Batsu asked.

"We don't. That's what I'm about to find out."

Batsu took a few steps closer. He examined the ice along with the look on Toumou's bandaged face, both raising much concern.

"Toumou, does it really matter? The caravan would never make it up the ice. It's either head down to the left or backtrack, right?"

Toumou tightened his harness and started to strap his boot spikes tight. "We don't backtrack."

A subtle sound then emerged. Batsu tried to make out the source, thinking it was coming from his own disoriented head. Between the banging of metal and ice, Batsu eventually deciphered the sound. It was water.

"It's already into spring, Toumou. Are you sure this ice is solid?" Batsu asked, feeling quiet sure it wasn't.

Toumou tightened everything down, pulled the retractable ice axe out from his pack, and finally turned straight into Batsu's questioning.

"You're afraid that your ambition might have driven you to promise something you can't deliver, a promise that might cost the lives of everyone here. We chose to cross here because the destination requires such a journey. There is nothing behind us; everything lies ahead."

Toumou handed Batsu his hat, took a look up the frozen cascade, and then drove his axe into the ice. He picked his foot off of the edge, carried it over the void, and then drove the toe spike into the ice. His left hand raised a second axe and took a swing. Picking his other foot off the edge and driving it in, Toumou suddenly hovered over a chasm of fog. The adventurer grimaced with every move of his broken body but pushed onward. The determination that Batsu admired earlier now made Toumou seem mad. Batsu nervously examined the anchor again to see if it looked solid. Deep within the ice, he started to make out the subtle refraction of light. The sound of water then became more apparent to him, like the serene sound of a late winter stream emerging from its frozen sleep.

Toumou struck again with his axe. In an instant, a fracturing sound shot out, and the entire slab of ice detached from the rock. The guide rode the ice down into the fog, which silently engulfed him.

Batsu stared down into the gray abyss that seemed to have suddenly swallowed up reality. He heard no sound, not a collision or a scream. He looked up to where the slab of ice held Toumou and his anchor seconds earlier; now, only a small stream of water ran down the rock wall. He stood there in solitude, his entire congregation of followers silently waiting for him behind the gray curtain.

Now alone in his role, Batsu came to a simple and critical realization: Toumou was right, they could not go back. Turning around would be accepting defeat, and they needed every shred of spirit they could retain. If members of the caravan could survive the Murde Mountains, they had to believe everything behind them had a purpose. Batsu then looked down at Toumou's hat. After countless journeys, the worn and softened leather now felt cold and brittle. He threw it over the edge, giving it back to its owner. Batsu then walked back into the silent haze.

The first person he encountered was Martouk. "Toumou went to scout something out. He wants us to go ahead."

"We're going without him?" Martouk asked.

"Gather the group. We're moving." Batsu spoke with the most convincing projection of self-assurance he could muster.

Martouk hesitated before deciding to follow the order. Batsu watched as the convoy behind him gathered its gear and began to line up. He immediately pushed Toumou's death to the back of his mind and gravely hoped no one would ask what happend; he hadn't the energy to lie to whoever remained. Having no knowledge of his final destination, Batsu assumed the desperate caravan would follow wherever he led; a successful travel plan had to be devised. He got out his compass and headed west.

Endlessly wandering through the field of fog, the mountain offered Batsu plenty of time to doubt any and all aspects of his grand pilgrimage. He had anticipated a few members might not survive the journey, and while most of the team remained, a sickening sense of dread sat firmly in his stomach. From below, the Murdes had looked like a gateway to the future, but up in the clouds they felt like a quiet nightmare, refusing to end. He felt his mind constantly slipping away to places in an environment where such a thing could not be afforded. At that point, any miscalculation likely wouldn't result in a trip back to the drawing board, but rather one into a frozen mass grave.

Time passed, and Batsu dragged his body forward, followed by everyone else's. He slowly started to slip into the thought that he actually wasn't leading anyone. Batsu imagined the convoy of people simply drifting through the mountains, everyone attached in an aimless journey. He watched his feet pass by the frozen rock for what seemed an eternity. The image reinforced his deteriorating mind of a truth that haunted him like the promise of death. As the mountain stood on the verge of killing them all, they still had an entire face yet to traverse.

Energy had all but completely escaped. People had died, and the Ice Cat managed to free the group of a few days' worth of rations. Batsu kept fighting an urge to calculate the remaining factors of their expedition, but the sum always equaled death. His head had drifted along for so long, that he nearly missed the first gesture of benevolence the Celestial Wall had offered. The gift, so subtle in its presentation, took some time to even be noticed. The path was actually sloping down.

The initial encouragement felt by his aching legs soon faded over what seemed like days of hazy light. Batsu felt his shoulder throb with pain and wondered if perhaps the Shiroku had killed him up on the ledge. He imagined his journey as a perpetual march, a walk through the hereafter.

Then, after countless hours of not even hearing a voice, Batsu suddenly felt a tap on his shoulder. Martouk calmly appeared. "So, Toumou hasn't shown up yet?"

Considering their situation, Batsu found Martouk's casual tone agitating. "No, he must still be scouting ahead."

Martouk stayed right behind him, step after step, like a dog that couldn't sense when his master wanted to be alone.

"I still feel it's worth the risk," Martouk optimistically stated.

Batsu did not make a habit of pondering Martouk's thoughts. "What is?"

"The end."

Batsu wasn't sure if one of them had succumbed to the altitude, or if Martouk had miraculously found the gift of poetry up in the clouds.

"Why do you say you still feel it's worth it?" Batsu couldn't believe he had inquired Martouk of his contemplations.

"Toumou died the way he wanted to, and so shall we."

The statement's biting truth crawled down Batsu's aching back. He could feel his chest tightening up. Maybe that oxygen deprived, endless fog would be the last thing he would see. Minutes, or perhaps hours, went by, and Batsu turned around to see if he had imagined Martouk; he saw no one. The air stood silent; not even the caravan could be heard, and he started to wonder if any of them even remained. Perhaps it was inconsequential; the path faded down into the fog, and all any of them could do was follow.

The hazy limbo became all Batsu knew. Energy had vanished, desire withdrew, and it seemed as though he no longer felt anything. The world, once seemingly understood, continued to dissolve into the eternal cloud around him. He waited for it all to finally turn dark, but dropping into the trickling madness, a soft wave of light somehow flooded his world. It seemed impossible, and Batsu wondered if he had truly met the end.

The light continued to increase as Batsu's tired eyes began to strain. He fought harder to walk as the light became almost painful to look at. Batsu wondered if it was euphoria, or perhaps walking into an afterlife that he had always dismissed. Eventually, the light became too much, and Batsu could no longer see. He took a few more steps and then fell to his knees.

Fear and pain seemed to fade away, replaced by a peaceful acceptance slowly washing over him. His senses reached equilibrium, and he felt as though his body floated. Tension began to lift off of him, and he could feel tears of release begin to well up. After a deep breath, Batsu then opened his eyes, forgetting that he had ever shut them.

From an endless world of gray, somehow a blur of color now filled his vision. As he took another long breath, the colors started to sharpen into an image. Batsu rubbed his watery eyes and saw something that could not have been real. He had dreams of his promised land: an oasis that could sustain all of the ambition he could throw at it. Vast, arable land, forests, and rivers covering an area with ample space to build and develop. The sight that lay before him looked to possess all of that and more, but it could not be real. With all of the haze floating in his mind, he knew they still had only reached the middle of the mountains.

Hearing steps quietly stop beside him, Batsu looked up over his shoulder, seeing Martouk gaze out across the valley. "I was praying you would lead us to a great land, but I could never have imagined this."

Batsu looked back over the vastness of the valley, which his eyes finally managed to bring into focus. He slowly stood up, his legs feeling sore, but feeling nonetheless. The two men stood there quietly. The rays of sun, the lush green land, and the pockets of vivid blue sky offered too much to take in quickly. Feeling secure on the ground below him, Batsu gave Martouk a look of confidence, one he hadn't been able to muster for days.

"Go tell the pilgrims, we have arrived."

2
PROGRESS

A world unto itself, it floated as a jewel in a river of thorns. The isolated land mass brimmed vibrantly with life, making it difficult to exaggerate its natural grandeur. Weeks went by before anyone in Batsu's convoy could go a day without gushing over the magnificence of their new home. Coming in from the frozen peaks of the Murde Mountains, the sight looked beyond ideal. Upon seeing it for the first time, half of them swore they had finally succumbed to high-altitude hallucinations.

As a place to live, Batsu found the valley conveniently flat, a rather surprising phenomenon considering the jagged terrain surrounding it. The richness of the soil gave birth to a healthy variety of wild vegetation. His first smell of wildflowers nearly made him cry, something that felt entirely foreign to the industrial savant. The elevation decreased gradually as the valley went south, eventually ending in a wall of mountains that could be seen on a clear day, well over a day's journey away.

The name of the valley actually came from Jastoú, who spent a short time studying linguistics before diving into medicine back in Meijune. When his eyes finally caught sight of the beautiful valley, the doctor flushed all his anxieties out with a burst of laughter, or as much as his exhausted body would allow. He looked back over the Celestial Wall and felt at a crossroads. Their journey seemed to be at a beginning and an end, all defined by their perspective of an immovable mass of rock. A life had just been left behind, and they were experiencing the infancy of a new society. Naifin—an end, not the end.

Temporary shelter quickly went up, and almost immediately planning began for their new settlement. Batsu became emphatic with structure and purpose, refusing to allow anything to develop without consideration to the greater plan. He would almost nightly gather all of the designers and plan out the yet-unnamed municipality to be. Living districts, pedestrian walkways, industrial concentrations, farmland; they all had their place in the grand design.

Tempering Batsu's feverish energy to start building immediately, the lead farmer Boro reminded him that they couldn't work if they didn't eat and drink. The water problem looked to be of little issue as a good-sized river flowed down through the middle of the valley, a combination of spring water and melted snow. A soft, brilliant blue, the water had an almost luminescent quality to it. Considering the source, it came as no surprise that it felt breathtakingly cold and tasted as perfectly pure. Not wanting to take any chances, however, Jastoú played it safe and had all but a few consume boiled water the first few weeks. By the time he declared the river drinkable, most people had already been weened off of the sanitized precaution. It became hard to imagine anything in the valley being tainted, as it felt like the incarnation of a utopian fantasy.

Boro had been asked to come along largely because of the work he did on alternative farming methods, seen during a series of demonstrations entitled *Farm of Tomorrow*. Technology expos in Meijune often served as a social club for the progressively intellectual, esoteric crowd; a place for those who obsessively chased after their ideas. The Naifin Valley felt like a sandbox for Batsu's artisan collective. It inundated energy into Boro who seemed to have a permanently affixed smile, almost constantly laughing. Two of his concerned workers asked Jastoú if their mentor had suffered brain damage in the thin mountain air. The good doctor assured them the symptoms likely resulted from experiencing an abundance of life after so many days of tasting death.

Both Boro and Batsu agreed that the farmland should be established upriver, avoiding any potential contamination produced from the onslaught of industry, something Batsu planned on unleashing farther south. Boro had managed to bring along quite an impressive collection of seeds but knew their test would be a lengthy one, especially working in such foreign soil.

Boro observed that the valley appeared to be encased in a meteorological bubble, a factor that could potentially ensure consistent harvests from year to year. After settling on the amount of land they would need for future growth, Batsu signed off, and Boro gathered a team to build his farm of tomorrow.

Eager to gather raw materials to feed his industrial ambitions, Batsu assigned four pairs to prospect the surrounding land. He intended to send them off packing light; food collection started slow, and he theorized the journey shouldn't last more than two or three days, including on-site time. Surveying the distant southern end, however, would take at least three times as long and require a third man to handle the extra gear. Wasting little time, he sent off the first three teams.

Two days passed before the first team of material surveyors returned from their trip to the eastern edge of the valley. Having traveled through that same passage upon their initial arrival, the team quickly handled the moderately familiar terrain. Batsu analyzed the samples they brought back before sending them over to the metallurgists, who already set up small analysis stations. The following day, two more groups arrived with similar success; only the southern team remained.

While some of the rock samples appeared more intriguing than others, the oddest sample collected originally didn't get much attention from Batsu. One of Boro's apprentices had candidly mentioned a fist-sized rock that looked like some sort of relic. Its material didn't seem to be of substantial importance, and Batsu initially set it aside. Once the explorers left Batsu to himself, the peculiar stone finally reined in his attention.

Taking a more determined look at it, Batsu began to see a form that felt more intentional the longer he gazed at it. He hesitated to consider it crafted, but it had an undeniably symmetrical shape. The figure did not look human, or like any animal he could think of, but it was some kind of figure nonetheless. The only distinct feature appeared to be a pair of downward sloping eyes, if one wanted to assume such a thing. Batsu looked out his window, into the hills from where the team had returned. Only then did the critical thought first form in Batsu's mind: They might not be the first ones to have lived in the valley. The land looked completely undeveloped, but what he held in his hand had undeniable implications. As his mind tried to envision whatever civilization made the simple object, a more troubling question pushed forward: What was it that made them disappear? He got little sleep the next two nights.

With things developing better than expected, Batsu finally decided to send a team to the south. Despite having little opinion of him before their mountain trek, Batsu felt Martouk had held himself together remarkably well. The young man's state of calm initially confused Batsu, as he oddly seemed to gain composure the more their outlook appeared beyond hope. Less concerned with personal peculiarities, Batsu felt Martouk had proven himself capable as a group leader. Since the young man also had experience working with wood, a much valued commodity, the choice became easy.

To complete Martouk's team, Batsu decided to go with the Kolair brothers, Loto and Meek. Chosen largely off of Jastoú's suggestion, they were promising mechanical and biological artisans, physically strong and mentally fit. Batsu figured any siblings that peacefully handled the trip through the Murdes should have no problem making it across the pristine valley to the south.

Once he had them together, Batsu explained the hierarchy of their expedition. "The fundamental goal for this mission is to discover what raw materials we'll have access to at the edges of the valley. Mineral samples are key; we'll need to know what we can forge and manufacture. If you see any interesting plant, berries, or something of the sort, take just a small sample on your way back. Jastoú or Boro might find some useful function for them."

"Or at least something that might make Nola's bread more palatable," Loto cracked.

Meek shot his brother a look, one filled with defensive embarrassment.

"What?" Loto asked, knowing very well why he had gotten the look.

"Just..." Is all Meek got out before dismissing the potential conversation and refocusing on their leader.

Batsu cleared his throat. "Do not eat anything you cannot positively identify. I don't want to see you coming back on a stretcher, explaining how you had to leave rock samples behind because you couldn't resist a little bundle of toxic red berries."

"Of course, absolutely."

"Martouk, I want you to see if the lumber resources down there are any different than what we have access to up here."

"You want samples?"

"Just nothing too heavy. You're the expert, so if you find anything notable, do that. And be sure to take along some kind of weapon; again, nothing too heavy but capable of dealing with one of those damned cats." Batsu felt an ache in his left thigh. "Any questions?"

The two brothers shrugged at one another.

Martouk kept his eyes on Batsu and asked. "What if we find something . . . very unexpected?"

Batsu folded his arms and began to scratch his short beard. He reminded himself to be open-minded about such a foreign land; for all he knew, some blood-thirsty tribe of mystics could be living in a cave down at the other end.

"If there is something more dire than wood samples to report, feel free to spoil the surprise sooner rather than later."

The three men nodded, collected their things, and left to pursue their mission. The progressive leader then looked out of the glassless window in his makeshift board room. He peered out and saw the bustling activity of a society taking its first steps. Temporary shelters went up as others got repurposed, making way for more permanent structures. Raw material fed into the mouths of small processing stations, forming the building blocks for whatever his design called for. Refining, mining, milling, assembling—everything working together as a burgeoning organism.

As a working practice, Batsu typically operated as an isolationist until his developments finished. Watching anyone, let alone the entirety of a small society working on his personal magnum opus, invigorated him in an unprecedented way. Simultaneously, it existed as the most personal and communal thing he'd ever been a part of. After basking in the sight for a while, he stepped out to get his hands just a little dirty.

He approached Boro's team, which attempted to work out transportation issues along with Pano. A somewhat delicate individual, Pano was an older civil designer who had semi-retired from a flourishing career back in Meijune; Batsu felt rather proud to have stolen him for his cause. Boro had just finalized plotting out the farming region and wanted to develop the fastest way to cultivate; then he would move the produce into the developing distribution centers. Batsu reminded everyone to calculate for expansion, a nonnegotiable design component. The visit felt a little ceremonial, but Boro and Pano still nodded with appreciation. Then, noting how hungry he felt, Batsu made his way over to the butcher.

He ran into Tamak's apprentice RóMean, who stood among the scattered butcher board, cleavers, and containers. One of Jastoú's apprentices, who had been discussing meat-preservation ideas, walked off just as the leader arrived. The amount of wildlife in the valley thus far seemed moderate, and they examined the option of ranching some of them.

The spicy smell of preserved meats made Batsu's stomach ache as he stood above a small pile. Calmly, he reached down and grabbed some jerky off of a plate. Wanting to project as an inspector, he subdued his urge to shovel the smoky treat into his mouth. The first piece seemed to be of quality. Wanting to be thorough, he decided to inspect a second piece before speaking to RóMean.

"How are things coming along? Do you think we'll be able to start getting some protein out of here soon? I must hear at least three people daily grumble about how long it has been since they've eaten a steak."

"Things are going good, maybe a little slow. I'm just trying to figure this machine out."

RóMean wrestled with some copper tubing he attempted to arrange into a box. The coil hooked up to a compressor that had a container of liquid next to it. All of the pieces looked well crafted, but their current arrangement left Batsu rather disenchanted.

"What is that smell? That's not going to affect the meat is it?"

"It's ammonia. We need it for the refrigeration unit Tamak put together. We had been using sulfur dioxide, but that is dangerous stuff to be dragging around the mountains. He thought ammonia would work, but didn't have much time to test it."

"Food is an immediate requirement. He should have found the time to test it. And the meat can't smell like this. No one would eat it."

"I hope it won't."

"What do you mean you hope it won't? Do you have any experience operating this?"

"Not really. Tamak ran over it with me once."

"So why are you fumbling around with it? Do we all just go hungry as you figure out how refrigeration works? Where is Tamak?"

RóMean suddenly went quiet. Batsu often had a hard time understanding the expressions of others, and the one before him now seemed particularly enigmatic. The silence quickly became awkward as RóMean failed to answer the simple question. Batsu's impatience broke.

"Dammit, RóMean, I've got things to do."

RóMean hesitated as if he had forgotten how to speak, until finally pushing out the words. "He died up in the mountains."

The space between them filled with discomfort as Batsu's stomach dropped. He hid a developing sense of panic as he tried to remember Tamak's face.

"Right, I'm sorry. I'm managing a lot of development right now, probably too much. I sometimes forget what happened just the day before."

RóMean made half-hearted eye contact before going back to the refrigeration unit. Batsu wanted closure to the situation; moody, ill-tempered workers generally were not efficient producers.

"Well if you need anything, let me know," Batsu offered. RóMean kept working.

Feeling satisfied with his consultation, Batsu headed outside. His eyes once again surveyed the bustling development all around and began to feel a certain sense of familiarity. Having been on a constant high since the valley first appeared through the fog, Batsu began to relax; the whole plan seemed to be working out rather well.

Feeling a rare urge to quietly ponder, Batsu headed over to the newly named Long Frost River. Standing on the bank, he felt the melted ice chill the air. The sounds of water washed over him, and he began to experience a peace so pure and simple that it felt rather foreign. Looking north, he saw that Boro and Pano had already activated a pumping station. The initial design would pump water into a system of troughs that went out to collection points throughout the settlement. Batsu considered the system *extremely temporary*, soon to be replaced with an underground network of pipes; everything streamlined and constructed to intentional standards.

Feeling confident in the handling of their more immediate needs, the Premier then turned his thoughts towards the future. His mind filled with metal and steam. Batsu headed south where he saw the towering black breath of his industrial child being born. Only there would his dreams truly begin to materialize, separating his progressive city from any other in existence.

While approaching the more robust portion of his congregation, Batsu took a moment to remember who, if any, of the black hands had died back in the mountains. The group of lead-neck workers were emotionally concealed but took strongly to disrespect. He held little concern over their personal feelings unless they affected their commitment to his vision. Recollection arose of Durbé as the only one who didn't make it; Batsu felt moderately certain no others had died, although the last days on the mountain were generally void of any certainty.

Large and dark, the structure Batsu entered hide the settlement's industrial heart. Just inside the entrance, he found Jastoú's nephew, Firéi, bent over a copper disk spinning between two magnets. Batsu had considered leaving the heavy, avante-garde device behind. Electricity was young as a practical source of power, but Batsu found its beguiling nature impossible to ignore.

Past Firéi, the prime development of power began to thrust into existence. Batsu joined a small team of workers wearing a fresh layer of warm soot; they had just finished creating the primary steam engine for his industrial garden. Witnessing it operate for the first time, Batsu became entranced by the pulsing mass of metal gracefully churning its powerful core around and around.

The engine had a single, one-meter piston machined under impressive tolerances. It joined a one-ton flywheel, ready to connect to whatever needed such power. A worker that Batsu vaguely recognized tuned it up with a large fixed wrench. The grand overseer reveled in the meticulous attention his creation received. As he watched the technician work, Batsu imagined second- and third-generation engines that would grow to incredible sizes. He envisioned men forging machines, forging a city which in that moment seemed limited only by his own ambition. Batsu's lust for progress was palpable.

Then a sickening jolt shot through his body as a thunderous boom erupted from the steam engine. The worker's wrench had gotten caught by the flywheel and pinned his arm against the support base; his screams mixed with the hiss of steam and stressing metal. Batsu's feet froze while an engineer frantically ran up to the worker. He grabbed the man's arm and attempted to pull it out.

"Someone open the valve!"

The man continued to scream in pain, the wrench digging into his forearm, slipping out of position. "Open the damn thing, someone!"

Finally, a mechanic ran up to the engine, the wrench slipping even further as the flywheel began to creep forward, bending the worker's arm. "Hurry!"

"I'm on it."

The mechanic started to rotate a bolt with a large wrench, trying to open up the valve so the pressure would escape. The engineer pulled on the worker's throbbing arm, starting to slip it out. Turn by turn, the mechanic feverishly worked the bolt on the valve. Then, a blast of steam came out, knocking him back. A second later, the wrench slipped and the worker's forearm snapped from the force of the flywheel. With a grunt, the engineer pulled the worker out, and they collapsed to the floor; the worker held his mangled arm to his chest.

Batsu had stood motionless the entire time. The engineer looked around intently. "We need a doctor!"

Batsu turned and ran to the entrance, stopping at Firéi.

"Get your uncle."

Shocked, Firéi stood blank-faced.

Batsu spoke up. "Get Jastoú, now!"

The command sent Firéi running up the hill. Batsu stood there, breathing heavy, his back aching with tension. He could hear the commotion continuing from deep inside the building. The worker's screams of pain pierced through the air and deep into Batsu's skull. He had waited there for two minutes when Jastoú arrived with Firéi. It felt like an hour.

"A man in the back broke his arm," Batsu pragmatically spoke after a deep breath.

Jastoú quickly ran towards the cries of pain.

"Get the foreman," Batsu commanded before following them. Jastoú quickly shot through the crowd and immediately tended to the injured laborer. As the foreman arrived to assess the situation, Batsu walked over for a conference.

"Do you think the engine is damaged?"

The foreman turned in disbelief. "Hey! I've got a man who's lucky to still have his arm attached to his body . . ."

"I have provided Jastoú, who will repair him better than any other man could. You are not a doctor and that engine is vital to life for every person in this society. Once again, is the engine damaged and, if so, can it be repaired promptly?"

The pulsing vein above the foreman's left eye slowly began to shrink. He reluctantly walked over to the engine and began to investigate it. One of the senior engineers bracing the injured man noticed the pair tending to the steam engine. He waited for Batsu to turn his concern back to the injured man, but the leader kept his focus on the wounded machine.

The foreman caught the glance of the engineer but quickly lowered his gaze as he turned to Batsu, speaking with quiet disdain. "Nothing vital. It should only put us a day behind."

"Good. Give the men five minutes after Jastoú leaves; then, get them back to work. Also, tell them to mind what they are doing. I brought every set of hands here for a reason, and I don't want to lose any more."

Fighting juxtaposing impulses, the foreman simply went back to the crowd, avoiding eye contact with the senior engineer. Batsu didn't bother to stick around. The sun began to set, and he decided to retire to his quarters. He stayed up rather late going over the designs for his city-in-the-making. Despite feeling exhausted, his mind raced too fast to allow for more than a few hours' sleep most nights. That particular evening, curiosity over the southern team's expedition kept him up. His tired mind began to fill with paranoid thoughts of crazed natives storming up to rid their valley of Batsu and his invasive, industrial dream.

Feeling like a fool, he then forced a more practical focus, trying to remember anything he had missed among his countless responsibilities. After a calculated dissection of his memory, Batsu let out a rare laugh. Having paid so much attention to every utilitarian detail of his municipal design, he suddenly remembered one of the more deceptively valuable components. He shot out of bed and began to dress himself, intent on immediately meeting with Chomi and Misko. Then, noticing the silence that existed outside, he reexamined his plan and forced himself back to bed. Not wanting to lose his thought, Batsu grabbed some paper and quickly scribbled down a short note: *The people need pleasure.*

∘ ∘ ∘

In the morning, Batsu headed back towards the center of town and looked for the settlement's primary performance artists. While planning for the logistics of the trip, he had made a very conscious decision to develop art and entertainment in the settlement. While only feeling the occasional urge for such a thing, Batsu assessed that smiling laborers tended to achieve better work.

Batsu found Misko and Chomi to be quite responsible, despite the fact that they were career entertainers. The undeniably eccentric artists had established themselves through a unique blend of acrobatics and humor. The eye-catching pair became further known for their vibrant, striped clothing complemented with ornate hairstyles, magically staying put during their routines.

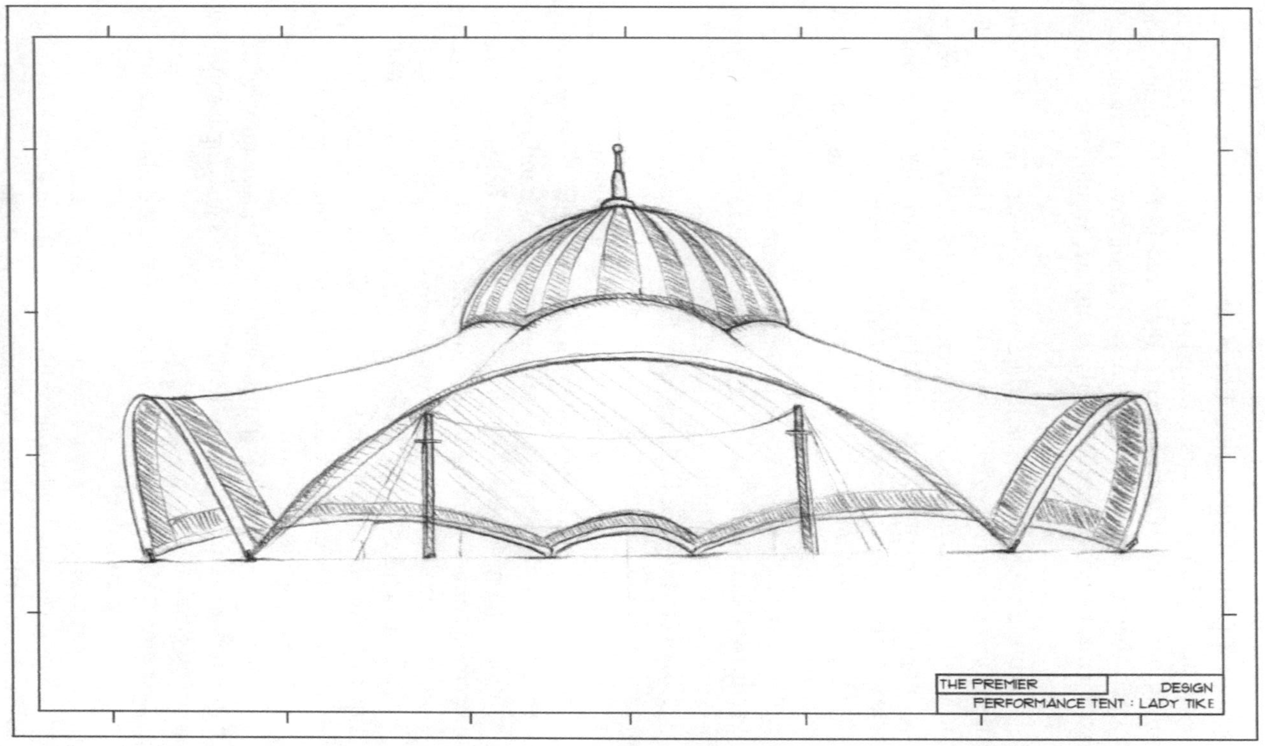

THE PREMIER
DESIGN
PERFORMANCE TENT : LADY TIKE

Currently they worked with Tiké from the textiles department, always known by her thick glasses and black attire. Tiké had been developing what she referred to as synthetic fibers, mixing some natural fibers with material rendered from chemicals. She hoped they would allow for increased flexibility and strength. A performance tent, already nearly complete, would be the initial large-scale trial.

Wanting people to frequent the center of town, Batsu designed the entertainment district right near its core. Upon arriving, he began to imagine a bustling society, collectively proud of its accomplished existence. Eventually, he found the entertainers hard at work and approached them with a raised eyebrow.

"I've been without a real laugh for weeks. I hope you can remedy that situation very soon."

"We had much time to conjure new acts on the way. I think it'll be a great while before we need to repeat a performance," Chomi spoke in his thick accent.

Misko chimed in. "Perhaps you'd like to be a part of our venue premiere, oh Great Premier."

"Not if you're trying to build a good reputation for entertainment."

"We all followed you over the treacherous Celestial Wall. Certainly you have enough charisma and wit to handle a one-act."

"Flattering as always." Batsu leaned in. "But between you and me, an evening of many laughs and little work could not come soon enough. I'll leave it up to you professionals."

"Well, I believe lovely Tiké will soon enough have a brilliant tent to house all of our work, and all of your laughing. Perhaps Great Premier would like to preview one of our new acts before the grand unveiling."

"Throw in a glass of spirits, and you'll make me the most content man in town." Batsu thought of how satisfying it sounded; *town, his town.*

"Chomi," Misko inquired, "would you please go find a bottle of something flammable?"

"Corked contentment at once, my captain."

Chomi ran quickly behind a few crates. Batsu already grinned at the rapport between the two performers. Misko began to walk towards the partially constructed stage, gracefully gliding with rhythm.

"We shall perform for you the story of the Great Premier. The enlightened gentleman of vision, who led a caravan of misfits to the top of a savage mountain and found the warm embrace of a majestic valley. A valley that stood bare and untouched, a blank canvas for which the artist Jean Batsu could build his moving vision. May I present to you, Valley of Progress."

Misko suddenly stood center stage, arms lifted high. At the same moment, like a cat, Chomi managed to sneak behind Batsu, presenting him a bottle of clear liquid on a silver tray.

"Excellent. I am parched." Batsu explained.

"Careful, Lord, this water might be broken and dehydrate you instead."

Chomi left Batsu with the alcohol and glided up to the stage with Misko, the duo making a rather handsome-looking pair. Misko took a few steps forward with perfect posture. Batsu took a sip of spirits and sank down into his seat.

"We have conquered the mountain and found the beauty that will embrace our curious lives. Let us build a city that will shine so bright, all of the outside will think the sun to have fallen into the cradle of the mountains."

Chomi followed up Misko by balancing on a small crate near the side of the stage.

"You have carried more weight than a lord should—or perhaps a woman could."

Misko lifted her chin and scoffed from across the stage towards her male counterpart. Batsu let out a cleansing laugh.

Chomi continued with a bow to his partner. "My sincerest expression of regret, Lady Misko." He then turned to Batsu while pointing to the crate. "But now that you managed to move this incredible mass so far, dear Premier, through a forest of treacherous snow and stone, allow this humble valet to move it a few more feet, so that we both may take credit for it reaching its final destination."

Chomi picked up the crate and set it in the middle of the stage. Misko then pranced over to the crate and sat on it with exaggerated femininity. Finally, she picked up a hammer.

"But your encouragement was more noble than the weeks of virtuous sacrifice, oh humble partner. Let me now raise my hammer to build this structure of progress; and if you could be so generous as to offer me your hand to guide this nail, I shall try my earnest to avoid tacking your thumb to its grand foundation."

Misko swung her hammer down as Chomi leapt to his feet, putting his hands behind his back. Misko, with the grace of a dancer, then chased after Chomi, who ran around the crate.

"But most gracious sir, I insist that you grant me the guidance of your beautiful and powerful hands. I assure you that any grief I have collected over the miles and miles and miles of carrying your entire wardrobe upon my back shall only be precisely taken out on the head of a male—oh, do excuse me, I certainly mean a nail."

Batsu continued to laugh, releasing the tension that had been building since disembarking from the east coast. His shoulders lowered as the performers continued to entertain in that improvised, private performance. Batsu felt warmth rise from his belly. Perhaps the spirits were at fault, but for the first time in weeks, he felt cozy.

The ambient sounds of the city developing around him became a calming, gentle breeze. It matched off well with the elegant and charming delivery of Misko and Chomi. The sound seemed to carry him off into a revitalizing trance, until something started to break through the phonic pool.

Loud voices surfaced from the south. Batsu turned his head and saw a few people gathering around a man that walked directly towards them. Although too far to make out who he was, Batsu could tell that a collective effort guided the man to the tent. As they got closer, the mass finally opened up enough for him to see the man responsible for the commotion: It was Martouk.

Batsu got up and began to walk slowly towards the approaching crowd. Misko and Chomi noticed his complete distraction and paused the performance. As they approached each other, Batsu then saw something odd in Martouk's step. He seemed to drift forward in a daze, not reacting to anyone. A chilling realization then triggered in Batsu's mind: The Kolair brothers were absent;

Martouk was alone.

As the crowd reached Batsu they quieted down, exchanging glances between him and Martouk. He waited for the young man to speak, but Martouk seemed to simply gaze straight through him. Martouk's skin looked pale, making his lifeless expression appear all the more ghostly. The small crowd sensed something odd and awaited their leader's response.

Trying his best not to raise further suspicion, Batsu finally said, "We have a bit of business to catch up with, if you all wouldn't mind."

The crowd quietly accepted the hint and slowly began to walk away, one at a time. When finally alone, Batsu took a step closer to Martouk and spoke, treading lightly.

"It's good to see you back safe, Martouk. Where are Loto and Meek?"

Batsu then saw some kind of reaction in Martouk's eyes. They began to widen, and a slight trembling washed over him. He said nothing.

"Martouk, they're not still down south, are they?"

Martouk's expression slowly slipped into a look of despair. His mouth started to open. Nothing came out at first, and then a faint sound.

"I . . . I think so."

"What do you mean? Did you leave without them?"

Martouk, still considering each of Batsu's words, nodded slowly. Batsu began to feel frustration bubble up from his gut. The wonderful mood he had just been enjoying was quickly sucked away. Martouk had proven himself to be a hardworking, trustworthy young man, and Batsu fought to give him the benefit of any doubt. If he left the rest of his team behind, Batsu theorized a good reason must have existed.

"You did make it down to the southern end, correct?

Martouk, again finding it easier not to speak, nodded quietly. Batsu could sense the strain on the young man's fragile mind. He leaned in, choosing the path of his words carefully.

"What is it that you found down there?"

"There was a valley."

"This valley, the Naifin?"

"No . . . it drops down." Martouk fought to remember. "There is another valley."

As Batsu took a moment, he tried to imagine the vague description. "What did you find there?"

An answer clearly rattled in Martouk's mind, but he didn't speak it.

"Think, Martouk! Is your team still down there?"

Martouk started to tremble more. He started to look afraid. "Yes."

Batsu cringed with frustration. "Martouk, what? What did you find in the valley?"

Martouk slowly conjured up the words. "It . . . was red."

"What do you mean? What was red?"

The young man could barely make sense of his own thoughts. Batsu attempted to fish more of an answer out of him without breaking the line.

"Was the valley red, the . . . trees?"

Martouk shook his head slowly, and then his trembling subsided. A spooked look of clarity finally washed over his face. He raised his eyes and looked straight at Batsu.

"They . . . they were red."

3
INERTIA

Although it would take at least a full year to evaluate, Boro eventually realized he had underestimated the Naifin Valley, truly an agriculturalist's dream land. The weather proved strangely consistent, so much so that it nearly led one to forget what bad weather felt like. The air even smelled comforting, nearly acting as a low-level tranquilizer. Jastoú and Batsu even noted how unexpectedly calm everyone remained when Martouk returned, considering his companions never did. The most problematic reaction resulted in hot gossip over Blashu Tea, the settlement's first indigenous drink.

Through consistent attention, Batsu eventually managed to get a more detailed description out of Martouk, but the story never felt complete. It festered a curiosity that prodded at Batsu like an insect caught in one's collar. The fantastical qualities of what Martouk tried to explain seemed nearly unbelievable, but the vagueness of everything had Batsu constantly working out theories. Batsu loathed leaving such a thing unreconciled in his mind, but he concluded they had no choice but to let it go for the time being. His growing city needed a focused workforce, and based on the amount of whispering that he heard outside, burning down the rumor mill seemed to be the first order of business.

Batsu ordered his followers to gather at Tiké's performance tent. Once finally constructed, it universally became considered the most eye-catching structure in the burgeoning city. Two large wooden beams held up the tent, topped off with a dome covered in red and white stripes; Tiké's synthetic fabric proved a stunning success. With the congregation bemused by circus architecture, Batsu decided to finally deliver his vague explanation.

He took center stage with Martouk as the people quieted down. He had no intentions of letting the young man speak, but Batsu figured having him there smiling and nodding provided sufficient representation. With a loud clearing of his throat, Batsu began.

"I'll keep this brief. I know some of you were wondering what the situation was regarding the expedition that went south. There are some details that are still being worked over, and I'm not going to talk about them here. When I feel there is something to report, I will not hesitate to inform you all. For now, and for the concern of everyone as a whole, I will say two things. First, based on the expeditions, it seems we have plenty here, and there is no need to look south for resources. Second, the valley is as pure and untroubled as anyone could hope, and we should just continue on with the work as planned. I know you all have plenty to concern yourselves with in your given area of expertise.

"This settlement has already proven that it will grow into a city and it will be great. But not only will it be great, it will be unlike anything the world has yet to see; something that will escape any modern comparison or even comprehension. Therefore, I decided it was time to give it a name: Primichi.

"Now let us continue on with the reason we came out here. Progress awaits."

o o o

It did not take long for rumors to start building back east about a city hidden away up in the mountains. Curious talk developed over Batsu's band of followers and what fantastic things they created on their island in the sky. Some suggested they never survived the trip, as no one had seen them make it through to the west side of the Murdes. Some suggested that they sneaked through, colonizing all the way to the west coast of the continent, or perhaps they circled around the planet and were expected to sail up on the eastern shore. A number of children concluded that they might have also turned into gods or spirit animals or something of the sort.

Batsu had expected such speculative, hot air to rise as it did for over a year. He disregarded it as an irrelevant factor until finally sending a small group back east to proclaim the truth of their grand success. Primichi grew quickly, and Batsu wanted to ensure an advantageously diverse society. The decision partly came on Jastoú's advice, something about the benefits of ethnic diversity and not compounding hereditary defects.

The returning group managed to gather over three times what Batsu expected. Desire for a promise land needed only the slightest sampling of truth to convince the disenchanted to uproot and embrace risk. The route up the Murdes still proved dangerous, but certain measures developed to ensure capable individuals to successfully traverse through along the established route.

Cables anchored into the mountain at more treacherous points, further leading to the construction of support platforms. Batsu felt proud only one life had been lost fortifying the trail. Better yet for the group, larger equipment became less crucial to transport as the young city already started industrializing on its own. The citizens of Primichi experienced relief when the new group arrived with no losses; however, Batsu simply felt validation. Another design, another success.

While still most comfortable working alone, Batsu felt the requirement of his responsibilities grew larger than what a single person could realistically manage. In the new convoy, two people emerged to work as permanent elements to Batsu's inner circle: a brother-and-sister team. Notably eager and confident, they exuded an aura of reliability.

Batsu didn't have time to get involved with all departments every day, so he tasked the brother, Joú, with going around the city, keeping tabs on development and updating him regularly. The sister, Clairah, would stay close to Batsu and help manage all that piled up on his lap. An extension of Batsu's reach, they would answer to him alone.

As months went by, Primichi's development continued rhythmically. Temporary structures phased out along with the imagination required to see where the city ventured towards. Its feet stood firmly on the ground, and Batsu finally released his firm grip on its entirety, if only just slightly. Moments of peace turned into occasional respite, allowing a shift in the relationship with his new business subordinate. Jokes sneaked into conversations, as did the occasional bottle of spirits during long days. It had escaped him earlier, but Batsu finally began to notice just how attractive he found Clairah.

While few people ever described Batsu as a romantic, Clairah found his passionate ambition to support the contrary. Although labeled incredibly bright, even at a young age, Clairah received little encouragement to pursue any field requiring intellect. She felt lost in her large family and needed little convincing from her brother, who wanted to venture into the proclaimed promise land; telling their family with a note they left behind. Batsu and Clairah equally surprised each other with how much they truly enjoyed working together, often sharing concepts and critiquing ideas. Their energies, having felt strangely unique for most of their lives, suddenly seemed to sing in harmony.

Almost as if scripted along with the events that preceded it, Batsu and Clairah became the first couple to wed in Primichi. The ceremony commenced at the tent that Tiké had built for Chomi and Misko, then going by the name of *The Premier*. The entire town attended what became one of its first formal events; not that either Batsu or Clairah demanded it, but it seemed appropriate given his status.

Since the constantly expanding city managed to miss its first birthday, Batsu's wedding became somewhat of a dual celebration. Although he appropriately focused on Clairah during the ceremony, Batsu spent the remainder of the evening celebrating their great city and gushing over its accomplishments. The new bride eagerly joined her husband, as neither enjoyed copious amounts of flattery or personal attention.

An apprentice of Boro's had taken up an interest in distilling local spirits and found the evening's celebration to be a fitting unveiling for her initial efforts. The first, an aperitif called Shumé, got a slow reception. However, by the end of the night, nearly all had found it highly agreeable. As the population hummed with jubilation, Batsu eventually sneaked off with his beautiful bride to their newly constructed home. Thusly, Primichi's first family officially formed.

° ° °

It took a number of years but eventually Clairah and Batsu managed enough time away from their perpetual enterprise to have a child. Although not the first baby to be born in Primichi, he was regularly referred to as its first son. Gaimen Batsu, the couple's only child, received an upbringing shared by no others. Batsu often used his heir as a way to gauge the new generation's perspective, a curious breed that knew no life outside the unique society.

Clairah became fascinated with her son's reactions to a life far different than her own, existing in a world of their own making. More so than Batsu, she would sentimentally muse on how they had the opportunity to create so many traditions to be passed on for countless generations. Especially during her pregnancy, Clairah became fascinated by the idea of creating an entire regional cuisine. Although her husband repeatedly swore the man had far more important things to deal with, Clairah regularly summoned Boro over to the house.

Known for its rich history with baking, Meijune's influence carried up into Primichi and, thusly, Boro developed massive grain fields. The wheat that grew there had a rather spicy and earthy presence and became a staple almost immediately. Boro enjoyed bringing over new crop samples to the Batsu family, sharing discoveries with their live-in chef, Izzy Kai. If any of his farmhands would ask, Boro consistently denied that his many visits had more to do with Lady Kai's curvaceous silhouette and big green eyes, even after they married.

Gaimen grew up, to no one's surprise, as a young man willing and able to continue on the path laid forth by his father. Despite his private confessions of being much closer to his mother, Primichi's first son committed most of his time to closely shadowing his more famous parent. Their public relationship became a symbol of prosperous harmony, quickly held up in admiration. Although Jean Batsu scoffed at the classification of nobility, his family comfortably accepted their ever-cementing place at the top.

As the city developed, its founders often mused on its superiority to whatever society they had left behind. Crime stayed impressively low, and transportation flowed smoothly along spotless roads and sidewalks. Regularly, citizens would congratulate Batsu on the execution of Primichi's virtues; but what seemed so unique in Meijune appeared more common up in the clouds. To the immigrants and creators of Primichi alike, the city felt like a haven for the enlightened; but for those who grew up knowing nothing else, Primichi simply became a new normal.

By the time another generation had come into existence, the monumental efforts made by those who founded the city slipped back, becoming known mostly through passages in civics books. The first social divide began between founders and the first generation, with both sides claiming the other as well meaning but misunderstanding. The gradual social development exploded into a collective discourse right as Gaimen's youngest son, Opaji Batsu, finished his ancillary school. The young man's active mouth quickly garnered attention, and a rumbling amongst the population began to unfurl. While willing to declare Primichi a fine city, he prophesied that something greater awaited on the horizon.

In what many would proclaim as arrogant, delusional, or downright insolent, Opaji took his entire inheritance, decades before the death of either parent, and foraged south. He ventured to create a new metropolis, a city superior in every way to the one that raised him. Waving money and promises about, he lured a number of eager or disenchanted citizens down-valley to start building where Primichi left off.

It quickly became known as the single most divisive event in the city's young history. Gaimen did his best to keep poised, but those close to him knew the father scoffed at Opaji's brash gesture. Some citizens wished the young visionary well, while many eagerly awaited to hear news of the experiment's miscarry; nearly all stood astonished at how quickly development happened. The one who had the most cause for offense, however, also found the entire event the least surprising.

Jean Batsu had grown comfortable basking in the existence of Primichi, but he never forgot the ambitious zeal that drove him to the city's creation. To the founding father, it made perfect sense that an heir, even a grandson, would be burdened with such a progressive vision.

Batsu, with wrinkled hands and a body much different than the one that scaled the Celestial Wall, sat still in a brass wheelchair. He watched his grandson's back as it faded in the distance, leaving behind the shining city that no longer seemed bright enough. After he disappeared, a glimmering tower began to rise far in the distance, vivid enough for even Batsu's aging eyes to make out. It became the final image he ever saw, a place claiming to be the most brilliant to have ever existed: the gleaming city of Chigou.

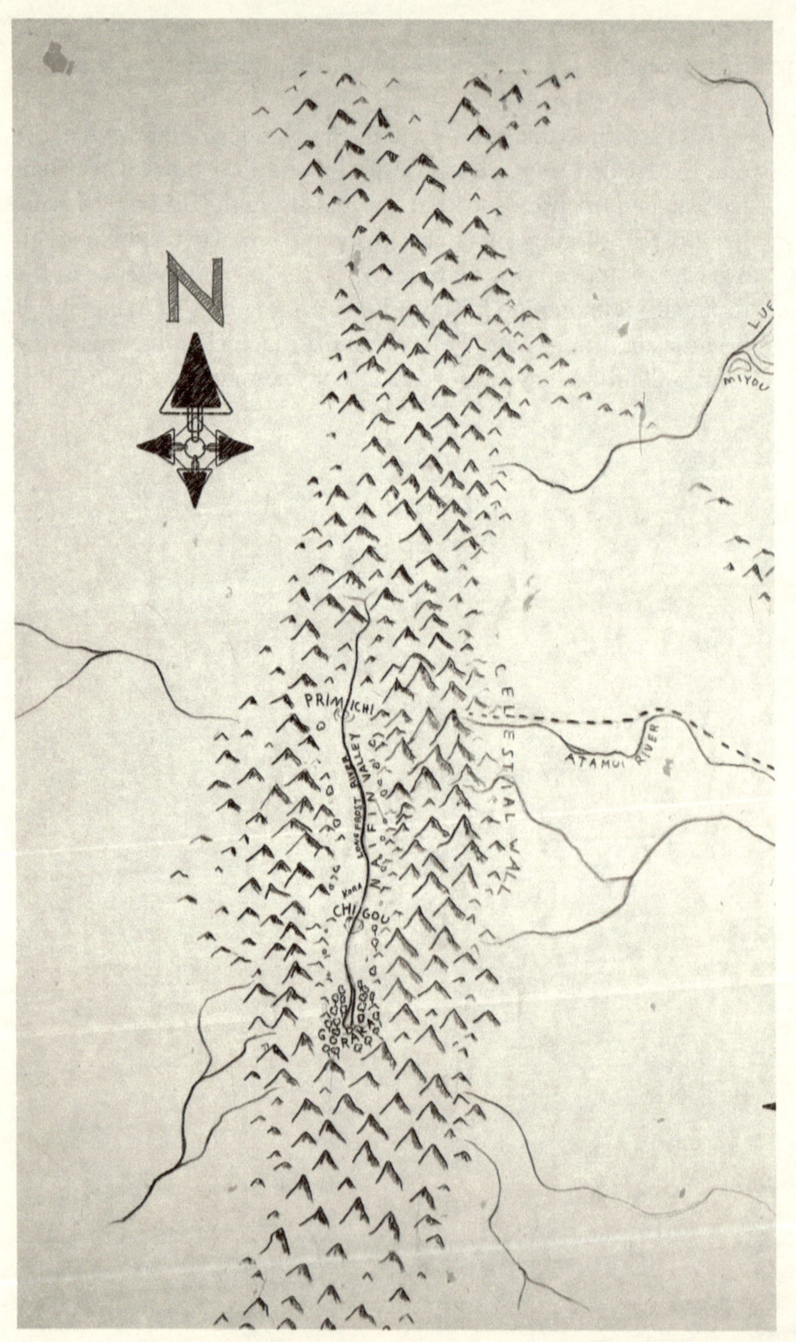

N
PRIM ICHI
LONG FROST RIVER
NAIFIN VALLEY
KORA
CHIGOU
CELESTIAL WALL
ATAMUI RIVER
MIYOU
LUE

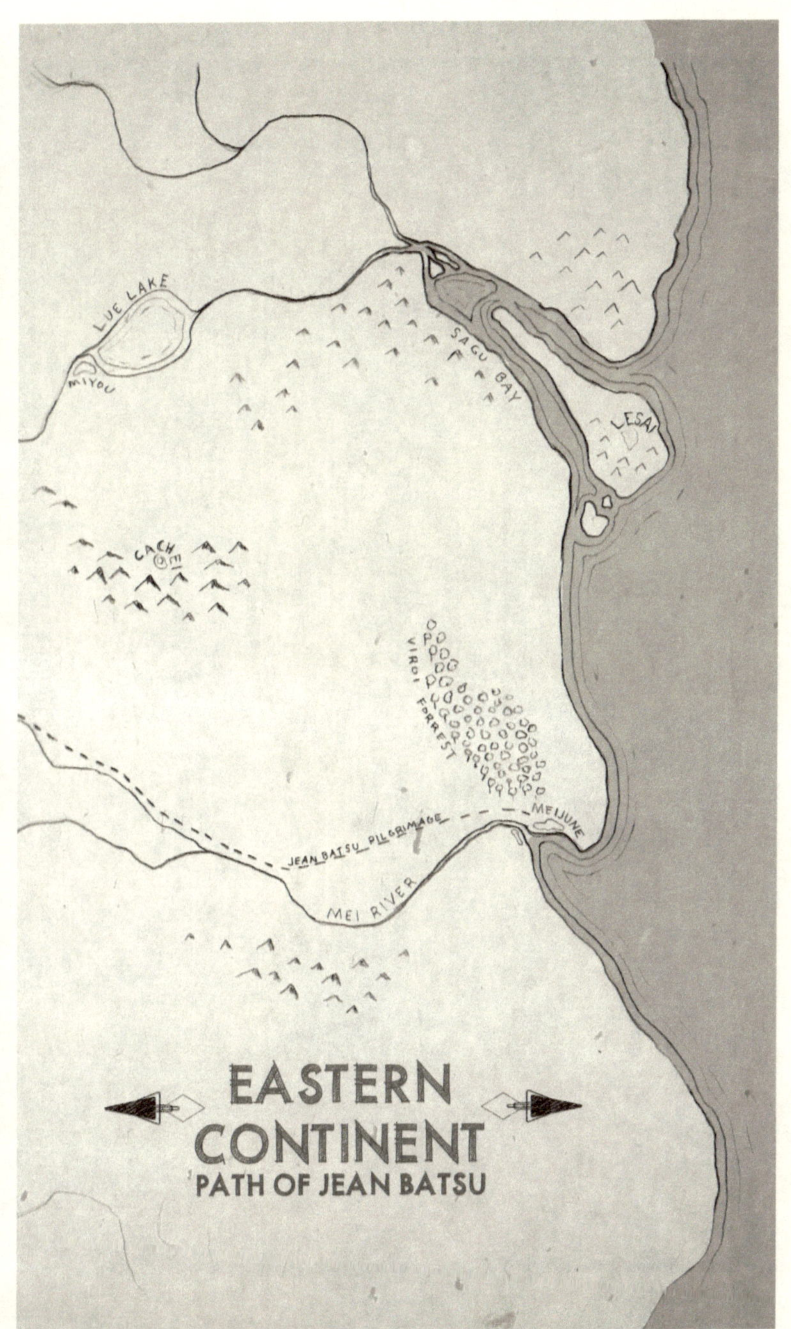

LUE LAKE
MIYOU
SAGU BAY
LESAI
CACH
VIROI FORREST
MEIJUNE
JEAN BATSU PILGRIMAGE
MEI RIVER
EASTERN CONTINENT
PATH OF JEAN BATSU

WELCOME TO
CHIGOU

Cory Sheldon grew up between the Cuyahoga Valley National Park and Akron, Ohio (an industrial curiosity, formerly the nation's fastest growing city). After graduating with an industrial design degree, he spent several years designing tires, directing films, and creating a movie theater. While teaching film and design at a local college, he decided to write his first novel, which turned into his first series: Valley of Progress.

Learn more about Valley of Progress online

MORE BOOKS · BLUEPRINTS · ADVERTISEMENTS
READING MUSIC · ARTWORK · MAPS & MORE

valleyofprogress.com